It is Freezing

by Rachel Russ
Illustrated by Bill Ledger

Houghton Mifflin Harcourt.

In this story ...

Ann

Ann is strong.
She can lift rocks.

Ben

Jin

Slink

It is freezing.
Ann needs her coat.

trail

Ben runs fast.

Ben cannot push it.
He stops and groans.

It is
too big.

Ann is strong. She can push it.

Jin sighs.
He cannot lift it.

It is not light!

Ann is strong.
She can lift it up high.

What is it?

Ann gets three bits of coal.

pat
pat
pat

Jin picks up six twigs.

12

Let Slink see.

It is me!

14

Retell the story ....